The Store Manager

The Store Manager

Robert E. Mitchell

VANTAGE PRESS
New York

This is a work of fiction. Any similarity between the names and characters in this book and any real person, living or dead, is purely coincidental.

Cover design by Polly McQuillen

FIRST EDITION

Published by Vantage Press, Inc.
419 Park Ave. South, New York, NY 10016

Manufactured in the United States of America
ISBN: 0-533-15459-6

Library of Congress Catalog Card No.: 2006900934

0 9 8 7 6 5 4 3 2

In loving memory of my son, Carl E. Mitchell
November 20, 1965–September 22, 2005

The Store Manager

1

"Not Arlington! He's not ready yet. That old man will eat him alive." Vick Noley stood in the store office talking on the telephone. He looked out of his mezzanine window across the acres of merchandise displayed on the sales floor below. "But . . . Jesus Christ. Why can't you send him to Ben's store? He would do just great there."

Vick seemed fidgety as he stood listening to John Holt, district manager, of M. G. Broad Stores on the telephone. The navy blue suit he was wearing emphasized his blond, thinning hair and fair complexion. "I'll tell him . . . yes. I'll have him there Monday. You bet! Bye."

Vick hung up the telephone and, from the mezzanine window, he watched Mitch Andrews work on a display below in the toy department. Tall and lean, Mitch was a dynamo emptying cartons and arranging merchandise on the counters. "He's going to be a good manager one day, if he gets the chance," Vick thought to himself. "Guess I had better give him the bad news."

A carton of toy guns was being turned into an imaginative display by the time Vick arrived in the department. "That looks great!" he said. "You have a knack for display."

"Thanks," Mitch responded with a quick smile. "It did turn out well, didn't it?"

"I've got some news for you. You're being transferred," Vick blurted, wanting to unload the bad news as quickly as possible.

1

"Where to?" Mitch asked anxiously.

"Arlington," Vick replied, trying to sound nonchalant. "You have to be there Monday morning."

Mitch's smile vanished. "That's where the trainee was fired last week, wasn't it?"

"Yes it was. And the two trainees prior to him quit—couldn't take it."

Mitch ran his fingers nervously through his light brown hair and tried to smile to hide his concern. "That doesn't sound too encouraging."

"Oh, you'll do fine!" Vick exclaimed, trying to calm Mitch's apprehension. "One thing I'll tell you about Nat Courtney, the manager: of the two hundred seventy stores in this region, and of the more than one thousand stores across the nation, Nat has the highest percentage of pre-tax profit in the entire company. That man knows how to make a profit. He's the master!"

"I'm sure I can learn a lot from him," Mitch said, trying to sound positive. "I don't mind working long hours. I'll work hard, and I'll work seven days a week if I have to—providing someone is not trying to run over me. But, I have no intention of being pushed around by a tough old codger with an inflated ego. I'll give him the best I have—and if that's not good enough—then I'll just have to be his next casualty!"

By the time Mitch got to the end of his response, his voice had risen considerably, and it was clear to Vick that Mitch was upset about going to work for Nat Courtney. It was almost as if he were ready to challenge him.

2

Mitch had butterflies in his stomach as he walked across the parking lot to the M. G. Broad Store in Arlington. He found the unlocked door which served as the employee entrance and slipped inside. The smell was familiar—like the first day of school when all the children have on new clothes. It always fascinated him to observe a store when there were no customers. It was like a giant closet with thousands of garments hanging in the semi-darkness. Nothing stirred; the only sound was his own breathing. In a few hours, the lights would come on, and the place would become a wonderland of color, customers, and activity.

Mitch walked slowly toward the back of the store. He looked almost like a mannequin that had come to life in his new blue suit, shined shoes, burgundy stripped tie, and white dress shirt. He studied the displays as he walked. The counters were clean and orderly; the presentations looked fresh and interesting. He stopped.

"That's awesome," he said to himself as he stared at a girls 7–14 coordinate display. Four mannequins were dressed in mix-and-match nautical coordinates. Nautical accessories of binoculars, sun glasses, cameras, and deck-top paraphernalia created a festive, party-like atmosphere.

Mitch entered the store office. Sitting behind a large oak desk was a rotund, elderly little man who could easily have been a model for a Norman Rockwell painting—bald on top, the white hair on both sides of his head was brushed neatly back. He peered over the spectacles perched on his nose and puffed on his pipe as he looked Mitch over from head to toe.

"I'm Mitch Andrews," Mitch said as he approached the desk and extended his hand to the man with the pipe.

The man stood up and grasped his hand, "Nat Courtney. Welcome to Arlington. Come on, I'll show you your office. When you get settled, walk around the store so you can see how I want it to look. I'll be back when the store opens to introduce you to everyone."

Mitch left his briefcase in the office and started walking the sales floor. The store looked like it was ready for grand opening. "Wow!" he thought. "This is one beautiful store. I'll bet Courtney is as hard to work for as I've heard." Mitch was still walking the floor when Nat came to get him to introduce him to the employees.

Weeks passed and Mitch wanted to make a good impression—get started on the right foot—so he focused all of his energy on his job. One minute he was in the hardware department building a display; next he was in ladies sportswear moving racks; then he was in the receiving department bringing out merchandise. He seemed to be everywhere.

"One thing's for sure," he said to himself as he was building a display of model airplanes in the toy department, "Mr. Courtney will know I'm not lazy. I get here early, and I stay late! He's certainly getting his money's worth."

"Mr. Andrews, come to the office please," a female voice announced over the public address system. He recognized the voice as that of Miss Tulip, the office manager.

"Now what?" he thought as he headed for the store office.

"Mr. Courtney wants to see you," Miss Tulip informed him as he entered.

She was in her mid-thirties, tall, plain, never married—the perfect stereotype of a spinster.

Mitch walked into Mr. Courtney's office. Neat stacks of purchase orders were arranged on his desk, and Courtney was puffing his pipe as he concentrated on one order in particular. He carefully checked quantity, price, terms, ship to, the ship date, and laid it on the stack. Then he looked directly at Mitch and said, "Mitch, you have a report due today on fishing tackle—where is it?"

"I'll get it," Mitch replied, and he dashed off to his office to find the delinquent document.

Mitch's disorganized desk looked as if someone had dumped a large waste basket on it. It was covered with purchase orders, memos, reports, merchandise counts, markdown sheets, advertising worksheets, and other unorganized information. He plunged into the chaos to see if he could locate the report. "How does he keep up with all this paper?" he said aloud. "There's so much here that I can't find anything."

While Mitch was searching through the mess of paper, Nat Courtney walked in. "What in the world is this?" he asked, and pointed to the pile of paper on Mitch's desk.

"That's my paperwork," Mitch responded, looking uncomfortable. "It's a little disorganized."

"Did you find the report yet?" There was a ring of impatience in Courtney's voice.

"No sir! Not yet! But I'll have it in a minute," Mitch replied, certain that it would not be that easy to find.

"You're not going to make it if you operate like that!" Mitch felt as if a bucket of ice water had been thrown in his face.

Mr. Courtney puffed his pipe and watched Mitch as he dug through the mess of papers, helplessly searching for the missing report.

"Come to my office," he commanded sternly, and he walked out of Mitch's office.

It seemed to Mitch like a very long walk to Mr.

Courtney's office. "Boy am I in trouble," he thought. "I worked so hard to keep up the sales floor, and I got caught on the paperwork." He followed Nat into his office and sat in the chair in front of his desk.

"You'll have to come over here if you want to learn something," Nat said as he motioned him to his side of the desk. "I call this my memory." He pulled out the desk drawer which contained a hanging file system, and he began to explain to Mitch how it worked. "I have folders labeled one through thirty-one, one for each day of the month. I have folders labeled Monday through Friday and folders for January through December." He re-lit his pipe and continued.

"In a store, you get hundreds of pieces of paper that must be handled in a controlled, organized manner. The paper contains information that is needed by other people to make informed decisions about merchandise and other aspects of the business. It's impossible to remember when each memo and report is due—so you must have a system! That system is what I call my memory. It's my one-to-thirty-one file."

Mitch looked at the files marked one to thirty-one, the ones marked January through December, and the ones which were labeled with the days of the week.

"Here's how the system works," Nat continued. "If I receive a memo from someone in the corporate office or regional office, and they are expecting a response to it on a specific date—let's say the twentieth of the month—then, I'll make a copy of the memo and put it in my file under the sixteenth. I'll instruct someone to gather the information and return it to me no later than the sixteenth. That gives me four days to get it in the mail and to the person who requested it. On the sixteenth, the first thing I will do when I come into my office is to check my one to thirty-one file so I can follow up on those things that are due on that day."

"That's really neat!" Mitch said. He was amazed at how

simple the system was—and yet he understood how it would organize his paperwork.

Mr. Courtney continued to explain the system. "Some reports are due on the same day each week. I put a reminder in that day's folder in my Monday through Friday file. For example, we do a zipper count every Friday—so, every Friday I look in that folder and pull our my reminder that the zipper count is due. Some things are to be followed up several months in the future, and I place those documents in the appropriate month's file; on the first day of each month, I look in the file for that month and place the documents in the one to thirty-one file so they will be handled on time. I can't forget anything. It's a great system."

"It sure is!"

"Let's make certain you don't forget it," Courtney said. "Take this piece of paper and write the following: I WILL CHECK MY ONE TO THIRTY-ONE FILE THE FIRST THING WHEN I COME TO WORK EACH MORNING! Now tear off what you have written and fold it into as small a wad as you can and put it in the pocket you carry your change in. Leave it there for a full week. Every time you put your hand in your pocket, you will feel that wad of paper, and you'll think about what is written on it. That will help you remember it. Now, you go get those files set up. I'll be back later today to show you how to set up your other files, but your one to thirty-one is the *most* important. Get that set up—and use it, and you will never be late submitting a report again."

"Thanks for your help," Mitch said enthusiastically, and he hurried back to his office.

It was late that night when he filed the last memo and pushed himself back from a clean desk. Every piece of paper on it had been appropriately filed. He was tired but satisfied. Mitch had learned something of value—a system he would use the rest of his life. "He's tough," Mitch thought. "But he knows his stuff. I can learn a lot from him *if* I can survive." He turned off the light and went home.

The next morning when Mitch entered his office, he noticed a sheet of paper lying on his clean desk. Someone had written on it with a magic marker in bold letters: I WILL CHECK MY ONE TO THIRTY-ONE FILE THE FIRST THING WHEN I COME TO WORK EACH DAY. He placed his hand in his pocket and felt the small wad of paper and smiled. Then he sat down and checked his one to thirty-one file.

3

"These slacks are the new, pleatless style I've been reading about," Mitch said to Ilene Markum, the men's department manager, as they were hanging the new shipment on a circular rack.

"I like the feel of the fabric," Ilene replied. "Wool and dacron make a nice combination. I'm going to the stockroom to get some more hangers."

Mitch noticed Mr. Courtney coming across the sales floor headed in his direction. He did not look straight ahead; his head seemed to swivel from side to side as he glanced first at one display and then to the opposite side of the aisle. Years of working in stores had taught him to inspect everything he passed, and he did it unconsciously as he walked toward Mitch.

"What are you working on?" he asked.

"We're putting out this shipment of men's slacks," Mitch responded enthusiastically. "This is the latest style—no pleats." He held up a pair for Mr. Courtney to see.

"We're a test store for that merchandise—let me know how well they sell. Do you have the white sale set up?"

"No sir. I haven't started on that yet."

"You haven't started!" Mr. Courtney repeated in disbelief. "You haven't started? The sale starts tomorrow. You'll be hard pressed to get everything set if you start right now. Why are you hanging slacks when you should be working on the white sale?"

"Well," Mitch started. He always said "well" when he needed time to think. He felt his face start to grow red as he tried to think of an answer. "I knew we were a test store for these slacks and . . . I wanted to make certain that they were displayed and monitored so we could accurately report on their performance. So I started helping Mrs. Markum hang them."

"Where's your coat?" Courtney asked.

"On the shirt counter."

"You always wear a coat when you're on the sales floor during business hours," Mr. Courtney said in a scolding tone. "If you want to be a maintenance man, you won't have to wear a coat. But, if you want to be a manager, you'll wear a coat so the customers will know that they're dealing with a professional."

"Yes sir," Mitch replied as he put on his coat.

"We need to talk," Mr. Courtney told him. "Let's go to my office." He turned and headed toward the back of the store, his head swiveling from side to side as he walked.

Mitch felt embarrassed and frustrated as he followed Mr. Courtney back to his office. "I can't believe I let the white sale slip up on me," he thought to himself. "Everyone in the store knows I'm in trouble. They're probably wondering if another trainee is going to get the axe." He proceeded to Mr. Courtney's office where he sat in a chair in front of Mr. Courtney's desk. There was an aroma of pipe smoke in the room. Mitch waited for Mr. Courtney to speak.

"How do you go about planning what you are going to do each day?" Mr. Courtney asked as he re-lit his pipe which always seemed to be going out.

The question caught Mitch completely by surprise. He had prepared himself to be yelled at. "Well—the first thing I do is check my one to thirty-one file. That has been a great help to me."

"You picked that up quickly," Courtney complimented.

"Then I follow up on those things that are due . . . and then I do my paperwork and mail."

"Then what?" Courtney probed.

"Then I go out and walk the store; I go to the stockroom to see what merchandise has come in that needs to be displayed—then I decide what I'm going to start working on. I work on something until it's finished—then, I find something else that needs attention, and I work on it. Mr. Courtney, I get a lot accomplished in a day—I don't watch the clock. I'm here early, and I work late even when I'm not scheduled. I do an awful lot around here!" Mitch's voice grew louder as he talked. "Mr. Noley was always pleased with my work." Mitch wished he hadn't made the last remark.

"You do work hard. That's one of your strong suits. I don't have to wind you up each day to get you started. You do that on your own. And you're right—you do accomplish a lot each day. I like that. I respect that! I know you come in early, and I also see you working late . . . even when you're not scheduled. Your work ethic will pay big dividends to you whether you work for M. G. Broad Stores or a competitor."

Mitch was pleased to hear the praise and felt a little less defensive. He sat back in the chair to get more comfortable. "But, even though you work very hard, you still are not as effective as you could be. You're working hard—but you're not working smart."

"What am I doing wrong?" Mitch asked, beginning to feel defensive again. He looked bewildered as he awaited a response.

"I can best answer that question by telling you a little story. Have you ever heard of Charles Schwab?"

"The tycoon?"

"That's the one."

"Yes sir. I studied about him in college. He was involved in the steel industry, I believe."

"That's right. He was the man who took a lot of small steel mills that were competing with each other all across the country and organized them into one powerful, very profitable empire known today as the United States Steel Company. He was bright, a good manager—innovative and aggressive. But he was also very frustrated. Somehow he knew that he was not as productive as he could be. Like you, he worked very hard. He arrived at his office early, and he worked late, long after the others had gone home. He tried to get as much from a day as it would yield. And he did accomplish an impressive amount of work in a day—but, he was not satisfied. He knew he could do more."

Mr. Courtney paused a moment, puffed his pipe to keep it burning and then continued. "He advertised a challenge: If anyone could show him a method or system which would make him more productive—more effective in his work—then he would pay that person twenty-five thousand dollars, a handsome sum in those days. Worth ten times that amount in today's currency! A very attractive offer, in any event."

"It sure was," Mitch agreed. His voice sounded calmer.

"When you make an offer of that magnitude, you don't have to wait long for someone to take you up on it, and that's exactly what happened. A man named Ivy Lee contacted Schwab and told him that he had a system which, if used as instructed, would make him more productive. Schwab agreed to see him and look at his proposed system."

"As it turned out," Courtney continued in a philosophical, story-teller manner, "it was a very simple system. Lee instructed Schwab to list the six most important things he had to accomplish that day on a piece of paper. Then take another sheet of paper and write the things in their order of importance. Lee instructed Schwab to always work his list from the top—so he was *always working on the most important priority!* If you're always working on the most important thing, it's impossible to spend your time any more efficiently or productively. 'I'll try it for thirty days,' Schwab said. At the end of the thirty-day trial period, Schwab wrote Lee a check in the amount of twenty-five thousand dollars, and he used the system until he died."

"That makes a lot of sense," Mitch said. "It seems so simple, but he's right. If you're working on the most important priority, it's impossible to spend your time more effectively."

"That's the point. Work smarter—not harder! You'll get more accomplished if you do. Schwab may not have completed everything on his list on a given day, but he felt a great deal of satisfaction knowing that he was spending his time and effort on the most important matters, and he was as effective as he could possibly be."

"That's a valuable principle," Mitch said. "Thanks for sharing it with me."

"I'm going to do more than share it with you. I'm going to see to it that you memorize it, and that you practice it." He took a sheet of paper and a pencil from his desk drawer and pushed it toward Mitch. "You need to write this down. 'I will take the first ten minutes of each day to plan,' " Courtney dictated and paused for Mitch to catch up, " 'so I can accomplish as much as possible in the time available.' " He waited for Mitch to finish. "Now, wad it . . ."

"I know the rest," Mitch interrupted. He was smiling. "I've been down this road before."

"I can't begin to tell you how important it is to have that sale ready tomorrow morning. Our credibility is on the line. People will read our ads all over the market area, and some will travel as far as seventy miles to take advantage of the savings. If we don't have the merchandise available at the price we advertised, we lose our credibility, and our customers may

13

never shop with us again—but what is worse, they'll tell their friends how we advertised merchandise we didn't have. It's a cardinal sin to advertise and not have the merchandise ready for the customers when they arrive. Make certain we are set before the store opens tomorrow!" he said sternly.

"It will be," Mitch assured him.

"You'd better get cracking then. You've got a lot to do."

Mitch hurried back to his office, wrote a list of the six most important things he had to accomplish that day, and then arranged them in order of priority on another sheet. At the top of the list was "Set up the white sale!"

Mitch immediately began working on the sale. He pulled stock from the stockroom; he moved merchandise from end-caps and promotional tables and replaced it with fresh, new sale merchandise topped off with brightly colored, exciting signs. When the store closed, he removed his coat and tie and continued to work on the displays. At three fifteen A.M., he checked item number one from his list and went home. Every display had been built, every sign mounted, and every merchandise count had been made. The white sale was ready. He was tired, but he had learned a valuable lesson that day—one he would use the remainder of his business career.

The next morning when Mitch went into his office, there was a sheet of paper lying on his desk on which someone had written with a magic marker, "The white sale looks great!" Under that was written: "I will take the first ten minutes of each day to plan, so that I can accomplish as much as possible in the time available."

Mitch slid his hand into his pocket and felt the little wad of paper. "It looks like he hasn't given up on me yet!" he said to himself in a positive manner. Then he sat down at his desk and began to check his one to thirty-one file.

4

Mitch was in his office going through the mail. He had checked his one to thirty-one file; his list of the six most important things to do was on his desk. He felt good about what he had learned, a sense of power at being able to keep track of and control so many things. Knowing that he was working on important projects also gave him a feeling of accomplishment and self-confidence.

Mr. Courtney stormed into Mitch's office. He looked angry. "Mitch, get out here on the sales floor, and bring a legal pad. We've got some serious problems."

"This is not going to be a good day!" Mitch muttered to himself as he fell in behind Nat Courtney who was walking with quick, long strides toward the front of the store. A stream of pipe smoke trailed over his shoulder as he walked into the ladies sportswear department; he stopped in front of a circular rack of coordinates.

"This is not acceptable!" Mr. Courtney stated in a loud voice as he pointed to an empty sign-holder on the rack. "What are we playing—guess the price?" he said sarcastically.

"No sir."

"Then make a note on your pad to put a sign in that empty sign holder."

He then walked to a counter of packaged blouses. Mitch could see the blood vessels in Courtney's neck expand. "What's this?" he snarled. His face was glowing red.

15

"Those blouses need to be straightened," Mitch said meekly as he added that to his list.

"You bet they do!" Courtney yelled. "And I mean quickly!"

"He seems to be getting madder," Mitch thought to himself. "Maybe that's how the others were fired. He started walking around the store and every time he saw something wrong, he got more angry until . . . he just exploded and fired them."

Mr. Courtney walked to a rack of better dresses and looked at the tag which was hanging from the sleeve. "The markdowns on these dresses are more than a week late!" he shouted.

"I didn't get to them yet."

"That's obvious." Courtney had reached a state of fury that Mitch had never seen before. "What happened to your sense of urgency? You used to have one!"

Mitch did not answer. He added "markdown better dresses" to his list. "No wonder trainees can't make it under him," he thought. "This is worse than a white glove military inspection."

Courtney stormed quickly into the toy department and stopped in front of a shipment of toys which were still in their cartons stacked next to the counter. "Do you know how long these have been here?"

"Yes sir. Two days."

"These have been here for two days?"

"I wrote the date on this carton the first time I passed it, and it has been sitting there two days!"

"What happened to the sense of urgency you used to have?" he repeated.

Mitch did not respond. He felt the hot blood rushing to his face and the burning anger in his stomach, and he wanted to yell back, but he held his tongue.

"I don't know what it was like in the store where you came from, but I'm telling you this—I don't manage a store that looks like this one. I never have and I never will!" His hand trembled when he tried to re-light his pipe.

Mitch concentrated on writing his list and controlling his temper-which was difficult. "He's right," he thought. "This store did not look this way when I came here. In my new-found power of follow-up and prioritizing, I somehow let the rest of the operations slip." The standards had slipped, and Nat Courtney had definitely noticed.

"When did we start displaying men's belts on the floor?" he continued sarcastically.

"I'll get those hung up." Mitch replied, trying to sound as calm as he could. He was thinking, "I have been so preoccupied with follow-up and priorities that I have failed to do the maintenance that I once did, and it definitely shows. I somehow lost control."

Mitch continued following Nat Courtney around the store. Courtney seemed to get angrier every time he came to something wrong, and he became more vicious in his criticism. "He is going to fire me for sure," Mitch thought. "I wonder if he will do it here on the sales floor, or if he'll do it in his office. Will he say, 'You're fired! Clean out your desk'? I've never been fired before. What will I tell my wife? She won't understand! God, I hope I don't get fired. I can always quit before he fires me. That will look better on my record."

"Do we sell shirts for one-armed men?" Mitch heard him yell.

"No sir. All our shirts are for men with two arms."

"Then why does this mannequin have only one arm? What happened to the other arm?"

"I don't know," Mitch heard himself say. "I'll find out what happened to it." He felt cold, and Nat Courtney's voice sounded as if it were in a dream, far away but very real. Mitch

17

had felt that way before in the military when he was under fire. It was a cold, unfeeling, mechanical response to the situation. The brain was expecting pain and had already anesthetized the body.

They continued through the store; Mitch was taking notes, and Mr. Courtney was yelling and pointing out every little detail that Mitch needed to attend to.

"Let's go to my office!" Courtney ordered, and he charged toward the back of the store.

"Execution time!" Mitch thought. "God, I hate to get fired! I can do this job if he will just give me a chance. Vick Noley tried to warn me. He knew what I was in for, and so did I, but I thought I could survive."

Mitch felt like a defeated soldier as he walked into Nat Courtney's office. The battle had been fought hard . . . and he had lost. Now Courtney was going to bring down his colors and raise the Courtney flag in victory. "I feel humiliated and embarrassed," Mitch said to Courtney, who was already seated behind his desk.

Courtney looked pale and hard, like a judge who was about to deliver a death sentence.

"Here it comes," thought Mitch. "The big 'F.' I should resign before he has a chance to fire me."

"What in the hell happened?" Courtney asked. "You were doing fine. Then all at once, the entire store went to hell."

Mitch heard himself respond, "Since I started working on priorities, I don't have time to do everything I used to. I don't have time to flit all over the store and take care of signs, hang belts, take markdowns, put up toys, and all the other things I used to do. I can't seem to get it all accomplished. You're right. The store didn't look this way the day I walked in, and I apologize to you for not keeping it up to your standards. I've worked hard Mr. Courtney; I really tried, but I let it slip."

Courtney's rage seemed to have cooled from "furious" to "very angry," and he continued his probe. "Did you instruct anyone else to take care of any of those problems?"

"Of course I have. But sometimes when I ask the employees to do something, it gets taken care of—and other times, they just don't get around to it. That's when I come behind them and take care of it myself. But lately . . . I just haven't had the time."

"You're not delegating," Courtney said.

"But I do delegate! I tell the employees what I want them to do."

"That's not delegating, and that's your problem."

"I guess you'd better tell me then what delegating is, because I obviously don't know." Mitch's frustration showed in his voice.

"Pull your chair around here and let's take a look at the list you made." Courtney was calmer and was talking to Mitch as a mentor.

"Now what's the first item on your list?" Courtney asked.

Mitch moved his chair to Courtney's side of the desk. "An empty sign holder in ladies sportswear."

"Who should take care of it?"

"Shirley."

"How long should it take her?"

"Ten minutes."

"Make a note to that effect next to the item on your list; that Shirley will accomplish it, and it should take her approximately ten minutes. What's next?"

"The counter of blouses that needs to be straightened."

"And who will straighten the blouses?" Courtney continued patiently.

"Shirley," Mitch replied.

"And how long will it take her to straighten them?"

Mitch thought for a moment. "About an hour."

"Then note it just like you did the other one. Next?"

"The markdowns need to be taken in better dresses."

"Who will take the markdowns?"

"Mrs. Henderson."

"How long will it take to mark down the dresses?"

"That's a big job. It may take a half day or longer," Mitch estimated.

"Give her three hours," Courtney advised.

"The toy shipment is next . . ." Mitch continued. The list was covered item by item to the end.

When they had completed their review of the list, Mr. Courtney pushed himself back from the desk, leaned back in his chair, and began to talk. "When you delegate a task to an employee, the first thing you do is to make certain that the employee is capable of performing the assigned job. In all the situations we covered on the list, we assigned people who were experienced and capable of doing what we want. The next step is to actually explain to the employee clearly and concisely what you want him or her to accomplish. And just because you told someone to do something doesn't necessarily mean that he or she understood what you meant. I have had situations where I explained to a person exactly how I wanted a display to look, and the person said that he understood; but, when I came back to check the display, it was totally different from what I had envisioned, and it had to be torn apart and rebuilt—a very expensive predicament. Was the employee to blame?"

"Not necessarily," Mitch commented.

"You're right. I should've made certain that the employee understood what I expected by asking questions; or, I could have had him repeat what he thought I wanted, and the misunderstanding would have been obvious. Doing so would've saved time and money."

"I think I do pretty well explaining things. I've had some

similar experiences where things turned out differently than expected, but I believe I've improved in that area to the extent that it's not a problem."

"And then," Nat continued, "you give them a specific time that you expect the task to be completed. That is one of the most common mistakes made by inexperienced managers. They think that just because they've told someone to do something the job will be accomplished. A specific time must be established for completion, or you haven't delegated at all. You've simply told, and there's a big difference."

"That's the piece I was missing," Mitch acknowledged.

"But that's not all," Courtney continued. "You must instruct the employee to report back to you when the job is finished."

"I didn't do that either," Mitch admitted.

"And," Courtney continued, dragging out the "and" to indicate that there was more to come, "you must go and check the task to see if it has been completed as instructed. Until you have done all those steps, you haven't delegated."

"You were right. I didn't know how to delegate, but I do now."

"You take that list back to the sales floor and *delegate* every item on your list. Report back to me at four o'clock this afternoon so I can check on the progress you've made. Any questions?"

"No. I understand what you want. I'll be back at four."

Mitch proceeded to the sales floor and methodically covered each item with the appropriate employee. He gave detailed, specific instructions, established a specific time he expected the task to be completed, and had each employee repeat back to him the instructions he or she had received.

All during the day employees kept reporting to Mitch that a task had been completed, and he would personally go inspect the completed work and check it off his delegation list if it met his specifications.

By four o'clock that afternoon, every item on the list had been accomplished, and Mitch went to Nat Courtney's office to report.

"Sit down," Mr. Courtney invited in a friendly tone. His demeanor was completely different from the man who had been yelling at him earlier. "How did it go?"

"Terrific!" Mitch replied. "I can't believe how much was accomplished today, and how little I personally did. It doesn't seem possible."

"You only have two hands. With those two hands you can work as hard as you possibly can, and in a day you can do a lot. But, I can take a delegation list and competent employees and accomplish a hundred times as much as you. You see, managing isn't doing everything yourself. Sure, it's good to show by example occasionally how to do something or to communicate that you are not 'too good' to do something. When the employees see you doing a job that they normally do, even if it's for a minute, you give dignity to the work because you did it. But don't do it for long. Delegate! That's the key to management, and, if you ever control a large organization, you must become a master of delegation. How did the employees respond to the way you delegated today?"

"Very professionally."

"I'll bet they were surprised," he chuckled.

"If they were, they didn't show it," Mitch replied. "They just went right along with what I told them and did exactly what I asked."

"Good," he replied. He was obviously pleased with the results of the day.

"It's time for another writing lesson, Mitch."

"Is this going to be a 'wad' day?" Mitch asked tongue-in-cheek.

"A what?" he asked. He looked as though he might have been insulted, but he wasn't quite sure.

"A 'wad' day," Mitch repeated. "That's when you make me write on a piece of paper and carry it wadded up in my pocket for a week." Mitch hoped he had a sense of humor.

"It's a 'wad' day, all right!" Courtney grinned. He pushed a pencil and sheet of paper across the desk to Mitch. "Now write," he ordered.

Mitch readied for the dictation. "I will delegate everything on my 'to-do' list that I can, so I will be free to work on the most important items."

"Anything else?"

"That's it."

Mitch tore off the writing, folded it into a small wad, and put it in his right pocket. "That was a hard lesson," he said respectfully, "but a valuable one. Thanks."

"Growth is always painful," Courtney counseled. "There's never any growth without pain."

Mitch felt better when he left Nat Courtney's office. It had been a hard day. "I'll remember this day as long as I live," he said to himself as he returned to his office. "That man knows how to get his point across. God, does he ever!"

The next morning, Mitch arrived at the store early. He was anxious to use his newly acquired delegation skills. As he entered his office, he made a mental bet that there would be a sheet of paper on his desk. But, he was surprised and disappointed to see the same bare desk that he had left the previous day. No sheet of paper this time.

"I guess he's not as optimistic about me as he was," he thought. "After yesterday, I can understand that. He had a right to be upset with me."

Mitch pulled out his chair to sit down, and there on the chair was a sheet of paper. On it was written: "I will delegate

23

everything on my 'to-do' list that I can, so I will be free to work on the most important items."

"Now that's more like it," he said. And he sat down to check his one to thirty-one file, list his priorities, and make a delegation list.

5

Mitch was making his early morning tour of the sales floor, preparing a list of things that needed to be accomplished that day. He felt good about his progress and how well the store was operating. "It's been two months since I've had a 'wad' day," he thought to himself. Things seem to be going great. I'm using my one to thirty-one file; I'm prioritizing my work, and I'm delegating everything I possibly can. I have really learned a lot since I've been here." He saw Nat Courtney coming across the sales floor toward him.

"Good morning, Mr. Courtney!" he said enthusiastically. He hoped it would be a good morning, indeed, and that Nat Courtney wasn't going to blind side him with a problem.

"Morning," Courtney returned. "How's it going?"

"Good. I'm making my to-do list."

"Time well spent," Courtney complimented. "Will you let me know what time Mrs. Bath comes in?"

"Sure. Anything in particular I should look for?"

"No. She's scheduled for nine-thirty this morning in the jewelry department. She needs to be there when the store opens. I've been reviewing the time cards, and I noticed that she's been punching in on some occasions as late as nine forty-five, and that just isn't like her. She's worked here for several years, and I've never had a problem with her being late. Has she been calling you to let you know she would be late?"

"No. I wasn't aware that she was late."

"Keep your eyes open and let me know when she arrives. If she's tardy, tell me as soon as she comes in." He turned and headed back toward his office, observing everything within twenty feet of his path.

At nine twenty-five A.M., Mitch slipped on his camel-colored jacket. It was slightly lighter in shade than the color of his hair and seemed to be the perfect match for the brown slacks and tie he was wearing. "Mrs. Bath should be coming through the door if she's going to be in her department by nine thirty," he thought. "She'd better be on time or that little manager will have her head."

At nine-thirty, Mitch walked to the front of the store and unlocked the doors. "Good morning!" he greeted the small group of customers who were waiting outside for the store to open. "Welcome to Broad's!"

"Where is the yarn that's on sale?" a lady asked.

"Go over three aisles," Mitch said pointing in the direction she should go, "make a right, and it's on the fourth counter on your right."

"Thanks," she said and hurried off to find her bargain.

The lights were on; the store was sparkling; customers were everywhere—but at nine forty-five, there was still no one in the jewelry department. At nine fifty-three, Mitch saw her come charging through the front door and head toward the employee lounge to punch the time-clock. He observed her from a distance and saw that after she punched in, she went to her locker and put away her personal items; by the time she finally made it behind the jewelry counter, the time was five after ten. He went to Mr. Courtney's office to inform him.

"She came through the door at nine fifty-three, but it was five after ten before she was actually in her department."

"You've got two serious problems on your hands then."

"Two?"

"She is stealing time from you, and she is coming in late.

Probably the greatest theft you will experience in your career will be *the theft of time*! It is so hard to detect. You'll see employees come in at the exact moment they are scheduled to be on the sales floor, and they'll punch in frantically, so they can be 'on time'—and then they change to a much slower, more relaxed pace. They go to their locker to hang their coat and put on the smock that they must wear. Next, they go to the restroom and spend a few minutes there spraying their hair or whatever, and then they casually stroll to their work station. After all, they were at work on time—the time card says so! And they're getting paid for all that fooling around. Scheduled for nine-thirty means that she is expected to be on the sales floor at her work station at nine-thirty so she can wait on customers." He banged his fist on the top of his desk to add emphasis to his statement.

"I understand," Mitch said.

"If she steals twelve minutes a day, five days a week, fifty-two weeks a year—why, that's eight days. Can you afford to give her another week plus a day of vacation with pay on top of what she already gets?"

"No sir!"

"You bet you can't. Now what are you going to do to correct these problems?"

"Me?" Mitch asked surprised.

"If you're going to be a store manager, you've got to learn to deal with all the problems, and that includes the ones you'll have the most of—personnel problems."

"Okay," Mitch said. "I'm going to tell her that she has to be here on time, and that means on the floor ready to work. It doesn't mean hitting the time clock and fooling around in the lounge for ten to fifteen minutes."

"Good. That addresses part of it."

Mitch thought for a minute about what he had missed. "And I'll tell her that if she's going to be tardy and knows it, she must call and advise us so we can get someone to cover her area."

"Very good! Now get someone to cover her department, take Mrs. Bath to your office, and let her know that her behavior *will not be tolerated*!"

Mitch asked Mrs. Haynes to watch the jewelry department, and he accompanied Mrs. Bath to his office. She was an attractive redhead approximately thirty years old.

"Please have a seat," he told her as he closed the door to his office.

"What's going on?" Mrs. Bath asked as she took her seat.

Mitch seated himself behind his desk. His heart was pounding, and his mouth was very dry as he began to speak. "There seems to be a couple of problems we need to discuss," he began in a voice that was not as authoritative as it should have been in those circumstances. "You were scheduled to be here at nine-thirty so you could cover the jewelry department when the store opened."

"I had car trouble," she replied. Her hand was trembling and she was unconsciously twisting the button on her smock.

"Not only were you late, but you took twelve minutes to get from the time clock to your work station after you did clock in. That is simply not acceptable. Nine-thirty means you are expected to be in your assigned department at that time—not in the break room." Mitch was surprised at how firm he sounded. He certainly didn't feel that way.

"I didn't have time to put my make-up on this morning because I was running late. It's been one of those mornings where everything has gone wrong."

"You've been having quite a few of those lately, according to Mr. Courtney. He checked your time card and told me you've been late a lot lately." Mitch was still feeling tense and unsure about how she was going to react.

She looked at him as though he had hit her. Then her chin

started to quiver, and her mouth opened a little—almost like she was going to grin—but only a little, faint whine came out. Then tears started falling, great scalding tears that splashed from her cheeks and fell upon her arms and in her lap. The crying grew louder until she was sobbing.

"Oh no!" Mitch thought to himself. "I definitely do not like this part of the job! What am I going to do now?"

"It's my husband," she sobbed. "He lost his job three months ago. He can't seem to find work, and he's been drinking. He comes home roaring drunk and keeps me up all night—then he sleeps most of the day. I have to get up and come to work, and I'm so tired I sometimes oversleep."

"I see," Mitch said sympathetically. "I'm sorry."

"Not only do we not have his income coming in, but he spends money we can't afford on drinking. I don't know what's going to become of us. It's so hard! It's just so hard!" She leaned forward, almost laying her face in her own lap, and buried her face in her hands. She continued crying for several minutes.

Mitch was bewildered. He didn't know what to say or what to do. He sat there quietly and felt very much like a heel. "I didn't mean to upset you so much," he said after a long silence. "I just want you to come to work on time and to be in your department when you're scheduled. It's very important for you to be there to take care of the customers and to prevent shoplifting."

"I know," she said sobbing. "I've worked here for four years, and I've never had a problem before. I'll do better."

"Mr. Courtney said you had always been very dependable in the past, and he was surprised that you had been tardy."

"Can I borrow a Kleenex?" she asked. Her eyes were red and swollen from crying. "I look a mess."

"You look fine," Mitch assured her as he handed a box of Kleenex across the desk. "Why don't you go to the ladies'

29

room and freshen up before you go back to work?" He tried to sound as cheerful as he could, but he really felt terrible.

She left his office with red, swollen eyes that almost matched her hair, and headed for the ladies' room. Her small frame stooped under the weight of her trouble.

"I don't like personnel problems," he said aloud. "God, how I *hate* personnel problems!"

Two days later, Mitch noticed that Mrs. Bath was not on the sales floor when he opened the store. He went to check the schedule to verify that she was scheduled for nine-thirty; then he stopped by the store office and asked Miss Tulip, the office manager, if Mrs. Bath had called in. She had not.

Mitch asked Mrs. Haynes to cover the jewelry department until Mrs. Bath arrived.

He saw her come through the door at ten forty-five. She was almost running. Her eyes were puffy, and her hair was unkempt—she had obviously overslept again. "Should I tell Mr. Courtney?" he thought. "If I do, he'll make me talk to her again, and she'll probably cry. I'll feel like a heel again, and she will feel worse than she does now. So what would it accomplish? That poor woman has enough problems without me leaning on her. I think I'll let it pass this time."

Mitch was working on a lay-away reconciliation when he heard the page over the public address system. "Mr. Andrews to the office," Miss Tulip's voice said through the speakers.

"What do you need?" he asked Miss Tulip as he entered the office.

"Mr. Courtney wants to see you," she said, and pointed toward his office.

"Have a seat," Courtney said as Mitch entered his office.

Mitch took the seat directly across the desk in front of Courtney. "It's going to be a long discussion," he thought. "He never asks me to sit unless it's going to be a long meeting."

"Did you notice what time Mrs. Bath came to work this morning?" Courtney asked. He was looking over his glasses and puffing his pipe as he waited for the reply.

Mitch had the feeling that Courtney already knew what time Mrs. Bath had come in. "Yes sir, ten forty-five. She was scheduled for nine-thirty. I checked her schedule."

"What did you say to her?" Courtney continued. His eyes were as cold as steel as he sat watching Mitch.

Mitch knew he was in deep trouble. Courtney's stern posture and tone of voice communicated that to him. "Nothing," he said, and he felt like he should duck.

"Why not?" Courtney asked. His voice was a little louder. He was like a bloodhound of the trail of his prey, and he would not give up until he had tracked it down. There was no escape, and Mitch knew it.

"She has a lot of problems," he began. "Her husband lost his job three months ago and hasn't been able to find work. In addition to that, he started drinking heavily, and he comes in drunk at night and keeps Mrs. Bath awake. Then he sleeps all day, and she has to get up and come to work. I really feel sorry for her. The last time she was late and I counseled her about it, she cried her eyes out. That's when she told me about all the problems she's having with her husband. I felt like such a heel. I knew she had overslept when I saw her come in this morning. Her eyes were puffy, and her hair was a mess. I knew she was late—and I also knew why. She had enough trouble without me jumping on her and making her cry again."

Courtney started to speak slowly, and clearly. His delivery was like that of a judge delivering a sentence. *"What you did was a cardinal sin!"* His voice and demeanor communicated to Mitch the gravity of his mistake.

The words had a "chilling" effect on Mitch. "I don't understand," he said.

"You observed an employee's poor performance, and *you condoned it!*"

"No! I didn't condone it!" Mitch defended. "I just didn't say anything because she is having so much trouble. And the last time I reprimanded her, she broke down and just bawled. I didn't see how it would do her any good to repeat that."

"What good did it do to let her get away with it?" Courtney asked sternly.

"I don't know," Mitch admitted. "At least she's not crying."

"Any time you see an employee who is performing at an unacceptable level and you don't criticize that performance, you are not fulfilling your responsibility as a manager. Your first obligation is *always* to the shareholders. Those people who have invested their hard-earned savings to finance the business you are managing. It's your moral obligation to protect their investment with every resource you have. When you witness poor performance or unsatisfactory behavior by one of your employees, it's your duty to correct it!" His voice, as usual, was considerably louder when he finished.

"Jesus, he's going to get mad again," Mitch thought.

Mitch sighed. "I'm really not very good at that," he said, and he waited for the dreaded barrage that he knew would follow.

"You'll have to learn to be good at it!" Courtney shouted. "If you ever want to be a store manager. It comes with the job."

"Yes sir!" Mitch said to let him know he understood. He hoped Courtney would calm down.

"You're management! Employees watch you with the unblinking eye of a hawk. They constantly observe what you will accept and what you will not tolerate. That's why it's so important for you to always give them the right signals. Do you know what you've communicated to them today?"

"No sir, not exactly."

"You sent a message all across the store: 'If you're late for work, it's okay—Mr. Andrews will get someone to cover your department until you arrive. So don't worry about getting to work on time—he won't say anything.' And that's one message that *will not* be communicated in my store," he said tersely.

"That's not what I did, Mr. Courtney!" Mitch countered, his own voice became more forceful.

"That's not the message you intended to send, I'll grant you that. But that's the message received by every employee on the sales floor." He leaned forward and pointed the stem of his pipe at Mitch. "What are you going to do when you have thirty-five or fifty employees who don't show up for work on time? Put a sign in the front window that says, 'We will open this store when our employees show up! We don't know exactly what time that will be—so please be patient'?"

"So you think other employees will start coming in late because I didn't do anything about Mrs. Bath?"

"No question!" Courtney continued.

Mitch could not tell whether he was very angry or just putting a lot of emphasis into his delivery; whatever it was—it was very effective.

"And God help you if you don't do anything to her, and you punish or terminate someone else for being tardy. Then you come face to face with the law! And if the other person happens to be a minority, foreigner, or in a protected group, you will expose the company to severe legal consequences. If you go to court, you will lose the case because when the Equal Employment Opportunity Commission investigates the charge of discrimination, they will find that when Mrs. Bath was frequently tardy—you did nothing."

"I didn't think about that," Mitch said.

"You must be firm but fair. That has to be your policy as a

manager. If you don't treat all the employees the same way and use the same rules for all, you will get into serious trouble—and you should!"

"I didn't realize that."

"You couldn't see beyond the tears!" Courtney scolded. "You have to think with your mind—not your emotions."

"I can see that," Mitch said, and he felt very foolish.

"If you pass a spill on the floor and don't get excited about it—if you don't point out that it is a safety hazard for customers and employees alike—then you have sent a message to the employees that it's okay not to get excited about a situation that could cause a serious accident. They will no longer clean up spills with a sense of urgency. Or, if you pass a display that is messy, doesn't have a sign, or that simply needs to be restocked, and you don't say or do something to correct the condition—then you will have condoned the condition, and the employees will think it is acceptable to you. It's the same with cashiers. If a cashier is short on her register, if a charge sale is not recorded properly or a bank-card transaction is not correctly handled, and that cashier is not challenged and instructed as to what acceptable standards are—then very soon you will have people stealing from you. You will lose money from poor credit transactions, and the profitability of the store will deteriorate. Any time my employees show up for work with no smock, I send them home to get it. They will not work in my store if they are not properly dressed—I will not tolerate it!"

"I didn't realize how serious my actions were," Mitch admitted. "I wasn't thinking clearly. I was concerned about Mrs. Bath and her troubles and didn't give the first thought to my responsibility as a manager. What should I do about Mrs. Bath now?"

"Write her up! You call her to your office. Have the paperwork completed before she gets there, so all she has to do is sign it. Tell her you think she is a fine person (and she really is), but her tardiness is not acceptable behavior, and you're putting it in writing that she must improve. Tell her the next time she is late, she will be suspended from work for three days without pay. And if she is tardy after she has been suspended, you have no other choice but to terminate her."

"But her husband is out of work. What will they do?" Mitch pleaded.

"That's not your problem," Courtney advised. "Your problem is that she is not fulfilling her responsibility to you, our customers, or the shareholders. That's your problem—one you can do something about. You can either upgrade her performance, or you can terminate her. As a manager, you don't have a lot of other choices. You can't go getting involved in her personal life. For one thing, you're not trained to handle that sort of situation, and the other reason is that it's simply not your job. She and her husband will have to work out their problems—and one way or another they will. Most likely, he will eventually get another job; he will probably reduce his heavy drinking, and life will go on pretty much as it did before this crisis came on the scene." He leaned back in his chair. "Any questions?"

"No sir."

"Now go see Miss Tulip and get a constructive advice form filled out before you call Mrs. Bath to your office. Have Miss Tulip sit in as a witness, and let her also sign the form after the counseling session. Cover the unsatisfactory performance with Mrs. Bath as professionally as you can so that she fully understands what will happen if she continues to be late. And make certain that she signs the document once you have covered it with her. Okay?"

"Okay," Mitch replied, but his response was not enthusiastic.

"Stop by my office at five o'clock this afternoon and let me know how it went."

"Okay," Mitch said, and he felt the weight of the task upon him.

"She will probably cry again," Courtney advised. He sounded more sympathetic. "There's nothing you can do about that; it will make you feel terrible. But you must remember that your main mission is to act responsibly—I hope I have emphasized that enough to you."

"Oh, I got the message loud and clear. There's no doubt in my mind what I have to do in this situation . . . or why I have to do it."

"Good," he said. "Now go make certain that Mrs. Bath understands what we expect, and what will happen if she does not live up to those standards. Then you will have done your job."

Mitch arranged everything exactly as he had been instructed. Miss Tulip sat in a chair against the wall where she could observe everything without being a party to the conversation.

Mrs. Bath was already nervous when she entered the room and took her seat in front of Mitch's desk. "I can guess what this is about," she said nervously.

"This is not something I enjoy doing," Mitch heard himself say. It was almost as if he was watching, and he could hear a voice that sounded like his own, but he was not connected to the drama. "I warned you two days ago about being late, and this morning you were tardy again. You didn't call to let us know; you just showed up at ten forty-five." Mitch paused a moment to let his words sink in.

"You're a very nice person, Mrs. Bath. I like you, and I've really enjoyed working with you. But your performance is not acceptable. If I had not put Miss Haynes in the jewelry department this morning to cover for you, no one would've been there from nine-thirty until ten forty-five when you finally showed up. Our customers would've been neglected; shoplifters could have carried your department off, and no one would have known the difference."

"You're right," she said. "I know what time I was supposed to be here, but I overslept again. You know about my problem."

"Yes. I'm sorry for the difficulty you're having—and I do hope it will work out for you and your husband—but I can't tolerate your tardiness. I'm writing you up this time. If you're tardy again, I'll have to suspend you for three days without pay; if you're tardy after the suspension, I'll have no choice but to terminate you."

"I've never been written up before," she said. "Will this be on my record forever?"

"I'm not sure," Mitch admitted. "I don't think so, but I will check."

Mrs. Bath broke down again and started sobbing. "I can't take it anymore!" she cried. "I just can't take it!"

Mitch didn't say anything. He just sat there feeling terrible and helpless. He looked at Miss Tulip but said nothing. Then he returned his attention to Mrs. Bath. She definitely looked as if she couldn't take anything else; she was stretched to the limit. But Mitch knew that it was really out of his hands. Mrs. Bath was the only one who could solve her problems.

"Could I get you to sign right here?" he asked in a voice that was usually reserved for funeral parlors—that soft, respectful voice one uses in the presence of the deceased.

She stared at the paper through red, swollen eyes and unconsciously brushed a tear away as she read what Mitch had written. "I'll do better," she said, sobbing like a little child who has cried too long. "I'll do better," she reaffirmed as she signed the document.

"I know you will," Mitch assured her. "You're excused now."

Mitch watched her leave the room, a very nice lady who had a lot of personal problems. He hoped that she would not have to be terminated.

Miss Tulip signed the document as a witness and returned to her office.

Mitch sat alone in his office feeling very depressed. "God, I hate this part of the job," he said aloud.

At five o'clock, he went to Mr. Courtney's office to apprise him of the result of the counseling session he had had with Mrs. Bath.

"How did it go?" Courtney asked and he leaned back in his swivel chair and gave Mitch his undivided attention. He puffed his pipe and nodded his head as Mitch unfolded the details of the situation, and he injected an occasional "uh-huh"—just to let Mitch know that he was listening and understood.

"You handled that very well," Courtney complimented. "I'm very pleased. There's a good chance that you won't have to fire her now. She's worked here a long time. I think she's from good stock and will measure up to the requirement. Only time will tell, though."

"I feel really depressed," Mitch confessed.

"It's not easy, but it is necessary. And, if she does end up being terminated, you'll have the satisfaction of knowing that you did everything you could as a responsible manager to try to improve her performance—everything you could to save her job. And that's very important!"

"I understand what you're saying, Mr. Courtney, but I'm still depressed. This is the most difficult part of the job for me to handle."

"You'll be a master at it in time," he assured. "Just don't back away from your responsibility."

"I think it's time for another writing lesson," Courtney stated as he pushed a piece of paper and a pencil across his desk to Mitch.

"Another 'wad' day?" Mitch queried in half-hearted humor.

"Yup!" Courtney replied. "I will criticize poor performance each time I see it," he dictated, "so the employee will know that it is not acceptable, and I will take the time to explain to the employee what is acceptable."

Mitch wrote on the paper, folded it into a little wad and slid it into his pocket where he would carry it for a week.

"Put a note in your one to thirty-one file to report on her progress in two weeks, if you don't have to suspend or fire her."

"I'll do it," Mitch said, and he left the room to return to his office. He did not feel as excited about this lesson as he had the others. It was naturally hard for him to upset and threaten other people. It went against the grain of his personality. Even though he knew it was right and had to be done—it was still very difficult.

The next morning when Mitch came into his office, he saw the sheet of paper on his desk. It did not possess the same magic this time. He picked up the paper and read it.

"Growing is always painful! Whether it's a little boy crying because his legs are hurting from the growing bones, or a young manager growing to handle difficult responsibilities—there is no growth without pain." There was some white space, and then the writing continued. "I will criticize poor performance each time I see it so the employee will know that it is not acceptable, and I will take the time to explain to the employee what is acceptable."

The depression gradually left, and Mrs. Bath was punctual. Mitch noticed that she no longer had a "harried" look about her. "I'm really thankful I didn't have to fire her," he thought.

Two weeks passed and Mrs. Bath was performing well. Mitch reported the results to Mr. Courtney.

"I know," Courtney told him. "I've been watching her. I think she's going to be okay, and it's because you were a responsible manager. You should feel proud that you helped her through what must have been a difficult time, and, at the same time, you did not lower your standards. You forced her to stand up and be the woman she should be, and she will always respect you for that—and so will I."

Mitch felt ten feet tall when he left Mr. Courtney's office. And even taller when he passed the jewelry department and saw Mrs. Bath, well groomed, happy, and apparently dealing well with her problems.

6

Mitch felt more competent after he began challenging and criticizing situations which were not acceptable. He took Nat Courtney's advice and criticized everything he saw that was wrong, and he would quickly find someone to correct the situation. He would delegate each task and follow up with a diligence that impressed the employees.

While Mitch was walking through the health and beauty aids department, he saw a bottle of lotion that had been knocked off the shelf and had broken when it hit the floor. The lotion had spread and made a large, slippery puddle in the aisle.

Mitch stood beside the spill and called to an employee. "Miss Gould," he yelled. "Get Willie out here at once! There's a dangerous spill here that needs to be cleaned up!"

"Yes sir!" she responded and quickly called the office to have Willie paged to the lotion aisle.

Mitch stood over the spill so no one could accidentally step in it and slip and fall. Soon Willie arrived with his cart, hot water, and mop, and the problem quickly disappeared.

"That could have caused a serious accident!" Mitch said to Miss Gould.

"Yes sir," she replied as she waited on a customer.

Mitch came upon a display in the ladies underwear department that had no sign. "Miss Harris," he said firmly to the department manager, "this is unacceptable. Please have a sign on this display by one-thirty and report to me when it has been accomplished."

"Yes sir, Mr. Andrews!" Miss Harris replied.

"Who is that man?" a woman asked Miss Harris after Mitch had left the department.

"That's our assistant manager, Mr. Andrews."

"What's his problem?" the customer asked.

"I think he's trying too hard to be a good manager. He just hasn't learned how to wear his authority yet. These young managers have a hard job."

"He could be a little more human," the customer said, and she continued looking at some European-style briefs.

Mitch's first indication that he had a problem didn't come from Mr. Courtney. It came from Tim, a tall, wiry, high school senior who was also a co-op student. Tim worked in the toy department, and like most co-op students, he worked hard because his school grade was determined by his work performance.

It was a busy Saturday afternoon, and Mitch was passing through the toy department when he came upon a counter of small wheel toys that looked like children from an entire elementary school had spent the whole day playing—little cars, trucks, motorcycles, fire trucks, and planes were everywhere. Mitch could not tell where one display began and another ended. They were all mixed together, and several were still in the floor where the children had left them.

"Tim!" Mitch yelled. Tim was two counters away assisting a customer with a bicycle. "Come here when you finish with that customer."

"Okay, Mr. Andrews."

Mitch walked impatiently back and forth in front of the messy counter as he waited for Tim to finish with the customer.

Tim walked quickly to meet him. He flashed a quick smile

as he approached. His dark hair was held neatly in place by hair spray. A nice looking young man—no longer a boy, not yet an adult.

"What's up?"

"Tim, this is unacceptable," Mitch said as he pointed to the counter and at the items in the floor. "See that this is straightened by three-thirty, and report to me when it's finished."

Tim's smile quickly changed to a look of anger. "It wasn't like that this morning. It was perfect then," he said defensively. "We've been very busy today. It's Saturday, and there have been hundreds of kids here. I can't keep this large department perfect on a busy Saturday."

"I want this mess straightened by three-thirty," Mitch repeated sternly.

"Yes sir!" Tim responded and began throwing wheel toys back on the counter with more force than was necessary. He radiated hostility as he worked.

Mitch could not believe Tim was acting that way. Tim was a good worker, very conscientious—and up until now, he had been very cooperative. "Maybe he has something bothering him," Mitch said to himself as he left the department and made a note to follow up at three-thirty.

The next incident happened in the fabric department where there was a big sale in progress. Customers were everywhere, and so were bolts of fabric. Bolts were lying all over the cutting table; they were stacked on other bolts; sign holders had been knocked over, and the department did not have the neat, well-organized appearance which they strived so hard to maintain. Mitch had never seen the department in such poor condition.

"Mrs. Tippet," he said firmly to a grey-haired, lady who was slightly overweight, and who was busy unrolling fabric from a bolt for a customer. "Have this department straightened by three forty-five and report to me when you've finished." He started writing on his delegation list when Mrs. Tippet's response hit him like cold water thrown in his face.

"Listen, buster!" she fired back. Her face was as red as a fresh sunburn, and it looked to Mitch like sparks were coming from her eyes as she glared at him across her reading glasses. "If you don't want to be running the fabric department yourself, you'd better get out of here." Her reading glasses were removed from her nose, and she let them drop—and they were held by a chain which she wore around her neck. She returned her attention to her customer.

Mitch could clearly see that she was furious. He didn't know what to do or say. He headed straight for Mr. Courtney's office and told him about the incidents with Tim and Mrs. Tippet.

Nat listened intently as Mitch described in detail the sequence of events in each situation. "It sounds to me like you have a famine on your hands. People always rebel when there's a famine. You can work them hard, pay them low wages, provide them with terrible benefits and working conditions, and they won't rebel if they are not starving. But, when they get very hungry and you try to push or drive them, they will bristle up and resist. They won't follow your lead—they'll revolt!"

"I'm not following you," Mitch said. He looked confused.

"You will," Courtney said confidently. "After the incident with Mrs. Bath, you really took your responsibility as a manager seriously. Even though it wasn't the natural thing for you to do, you began to focus on 'less than acceptable performance,' and I commend you for using the 'firm but fair' philosophy. From what I have seen, you've treated everyone equally—no favorites, and no exceptions."

"I thought I was doing great!" Mitch exclaimed. "I really felt like I was on top of everything."

"No question that you were. Your performance as a manager has improved. You're using your organization the way you should. That's not your problem."

"I didn't think so. But I know I'm doing something wrong. People are starting to dislike me—I'm not trying to win a popularity contest, but I shouldn't be getting hostility from my employees either."

"Let's imagine that you are a co-op student who works in the toy department. You like your job, your boss, and you're doing well in school. Then, your boss becomes very strict, he gives you more and more to do and limited time frames to accomplish the work in. You work very hard to try to please him, but every time you finish an assignment, he says nothing—unless there's something wrong with it. In fact, the only feedback he gives you is criticism. How would you feel?"

"Probably like I was not appreciated."

"You bet! And you would eventually begin to feel like you were not doing a good job. After a while, you would start to think that he didn't think you were doing a good job, and that would make you unhappy. Finally you would start to resent your boss because you would develop the attitude, 'Why should I break my back? He never appreciates my work. All he ever does is criticize me.' When that happens, performance drops, loyalty stops and the relationship changes from supportive to adversarial. Leadership becomes non-existent."

"Is that what I'm doing? Too much criticism?"

"No, not at all. I expect you to maintain the high standards we've established. You can't back off from that."

"What's wrong then?"

"If someone criticizes you, how long will you remember it?"

"Well, I'm pretty sensitive. If the criticism was very harsh, or if it embarrassed me—especially in front of others—I would probably remember it forever."

"Most people are that way," Courtney continued. "Now, let's suppose you had done a good job in the toy department. You built a terrific display of plush toys, and your boss came by and really liked it. He praised you enthusiastically for your fine work. How long would you remember that?"

"It would make me feel good. I like positive strokes, but I wouldn't remember it for long."

"You see, negative criticism is so much more powerful than positive feedback. If you always give negative, pretty soon the people begin to hunger for some positive praise. They need it so they know they're pleasing you and that they're doing okay. When all they get is negative, they start developing a negative attitude, and their hunger will reach such proportions that they will leave to go somewhere else to get that need satisfied. People like to do a good job! They like to feel good about their work and themselves, and when they don't—they become unhappy and their performance starts to deteriorate."

"So I haven't been giving enough positive feedback?"

"Based on what I have been hearing from the employees, you haven't been giving any. And sometimes your expectations are unrealistic. You can't expect to accomplish the impossible."

"You're right. I used to be more considerate when I first started. I did praise more then, but I lost it somewhere along the way."

"Since negative feedback is so much more powerful than positive, you need to use a ratio of three-to-one. Three positives to one negative. If you had been doing that with Tim in the toy department, he would've been much less defensive when you criticized his small wheel counter. Another benefit of giving positive feedback is that when the employee is told what you like, he is much more likely to repeat that performance again because he knows what you want."

"Who determined that three-to-one was the correct ratio?" Mitch asked.

"I did! The hard way. It took me years to learn how to do it effectively. But it does work. If you are ever to be a great manager or a great leader, you will have to master the art of three-to-one. If you want to inspire, motivate, and develop people; if you want to help them be productive and happy; if you want to see them grow, then you must praise their good performance when you see it."

"So if I start telling the employees that they are doing a good job, they will be more receptive to my criticism."

"Wrong! They will ask you for a raise. If all I ever do is tell you you're doing a good job, then you'll think, 'If I'm doing such a good job, why don't you give me a raise?' You must praise the *performance*—not the performer. 'This performance is great; I really like the way you handled that display, etc. The performance."

"Okay! I've got it. I can see the difference. But what if you have an employee who doesn't deserve the three-to-one. Maybe a new employee who messes up a lot, or someone who just isn't as swift as the average person?"

"Then you'll have to spend extra time and effort with that person until he is brought up to your level of expectation, or you'll have to replace the person with someone who can do the job. Everyone can't work in a store. If someone can't, it's better if we don't waste their time and ours. We should make a firm but fair decision."

"Every time I think I'm getting on top of my job, it seems to fall apart. Something always happens that I didn't anticipate."

"And it always will," Nat assured him. "The way man learns is to try, to fail, to adjust, and to try again. And he learns from the process. You can't make a mistake I haven't already made decades ago. Don't be afraid of making mistakes. They are the stepping stones to knowledge. The people I can't afford to have working for me are those who don't make mistakes!"

"Because they are too expensive?"

"No, because they don't do anything." He chuckled. "I think it's time for another 'wad' day, as you put it."

Mitch flipped the page he was using for a delegation list and waited for Mr. Courtney to begin to dictate.

"I will praise good performance so my employees will know that their work is good, and they will repeat the performance because they know what is expected and appreciated."

Mitch wrote as he was instructed, tore the paper, and wadded it into a little ball. He slipped it into his pocket.

"Remember, Mitch, if you're ever going to be a great manager," Nat said, puffing his pipe as he talked, "that one principle will help you more than any I know. You practice three-to-one, and people will do almost anything you ask—and they will perform with enthusiasm. People live to be recognized and appreciated, and those few who have the skills to do it professionally and sincerely are the true leaders in business."

"Thanks," Mitch said. "I hope someday I can be as wise as you—and as good a manager."

"You probably won't be," Courtney said with a chuckle. "But don't stop trying. You may surprise yourself and surpass my accomplishments."

Mitch put three-to one to work that very day, and he was amazed at the difference it made. The employees had been starving for praise. "How did I let that happen?" he asked himself. "How could I have been so stupid?"

He passed Mrs. Greene who was busy stacking towels on an end cap. The folds were perfect, and the display was exciting. She had used complimentary colors to add vitality to the presentation.

"That's a beautiful display," he commented to her. "I especially like the way you used the colors to make it exciting."

"Thank you, Mr. Andrews," she beamed a bright smile and continued working.

When Mitch entered his office the next morning he was half expecting to see a sheet of paper on his desk. When it wasn't there he looked in his chair. It was not there. "I guess he forgot this time," he thought.

Mitch sat down at his desk and pulled a stack of papers from his one to thirty-one file and started skimming through them. He made notes on his to-do list. Then, he came across a sheet of paper on which someone had written with a magic marker: "I will praise good performance so that my employes will know that their work is good, and they will repeat the performance because they know what is expected and appreciated."

"He didn't forget after all." Mitch looked up at the wall directly in front of his desk. There, on a sign-board, was printed in large block letters six inches high three to one. "I guess he trusted me to remember that one," Mitch thought. "I didn't have to carry it around in my pocket to remember it, so why did he put it on a sign?"

7

Business was incredible! The store was having a banner year. Fresh, exciting new merchandise was arriving in the store and being turned into beautiful, imaginative displays which enticed the customers to buy. The organization was stable, for the most part, and was comprised of good, hardworking, loyal people who were happy and productive.

Mitch was progressing very well in his training program. He was ahead of schedule on his tests and projects, and Mr. Courtney seemed to be pleased with his performance. The employees had become cooperative and supportive since Mitch had begun using the three-to-one program. But Mitch started to feel uneasy. It seemed like every time he started feeling comfortable in his role of assistant manager, he was always hit blind side by a problem and ended up carrying a wad of paper around in his pocket for a week as a reminder to not be so stupid.

His first clue that life was not going to be perfect came from Mrs. Johnson, a sweet, enthusiastic, slightly heavy lady who was in her late fifties. Her hair was almost completely white, but she had the enthusiasm and vitality of a teenager. She was the perfect person for the candy department.

"Mr. Andrews, could I see you for a minute?" she called to him as he was passing her area.

"Sure. What do you need?" He approached her display cases loaded with delicious candies of every imaginable kind.

"What are you going to do about homecoming night?"

"Are you asking me for a date?" he teased.

"No. Seriously, one week from Friday is homecoming for the local high school. There's a football game, and afterward there's going to be a dance. Most of our students will want off to attend. I hate to tell you, but we'll be short of help on a busy Friday night without those students."

"Thanks for warning me," Mitch said. "I had better discuss this with Mr. Courtney. Sounds like we have a real problem brewing. By the way, your candy sales are terrific! You had a twenty-five percent increase in sales last month. That's impressive!"

"Thanks," Mrs. Johnson replied. She loved the praise, and it seemed to spark even more enthusiasm. "We're featuring pecan divinity this week. You should take some home to your wife," she said with a mischievous grin. "Maybe she'll be nice to you."

"That's a good idea," Mitch replied laughing. He caught her subtle meaning. "Weigh me a half pound—she just might."

Mitch went to Mr. Courtney's office to discuss the upcoming problem with the students. He described to Mr. Courtney the number of students, the areas of the store in which they worked, and the possible impact to service and overtime costs. He asked Mr. Courtney's advice on how to successfully handle it.

Courtney thought about the problem for a minute and then asked, "What's your first responsibility?"

"My first responsibility is to the shareholders who own stock in the company. They actually own the store."

"Right. Now what if there's no way you can let all of those students off to go to the game and the dance without hurting the store? If you let them all go, customer service will suffer—or profits will diminish because you will have to pay overtime to full-time workers who will have to work instead of them."

"Then they'll just have to work," Mitch concluded.

"Right again. But you would like to let as many as you possibly can attend, as long as it doesn't hurt the store, customer service, or other employees?"

"That's what I'd like to do." Mitch acknowledged.

"Then how can we accomplish that?" Courtney asked.

"That's why I came to you. I figured you'd probably handled this and similar situations before, and already knew the correct way to deal with it."

"I do," he said, "but I'd like to see how you handle the problem. You may think of a solution that never occurred to me. I always learn from the trainees who work for me. They always manage to teach me something I didn't know."

"Well, maybe if some of the full-time employees could exchange hours with the students who wanted to attend . . . that would work. The full-time employees would not go into overtime because of the exchange of hours, and the students could have the evening off to go to the homecoming event."

"How are you going to accomplish that?"

"We could pose the problem and the solution to the employees at the Saturday morning store meeting and ask for volunteers. That way, we wouldn't be forcing people who normally are off Friday night to work. It would be their decision."

"That might work," Courtney agreed. "Post a notice above the time clock that there will be a store meeting Saturday morning at eight A.M., and one of the topics we will discuss will be the upcoming homecoming."

"I'll post it at once." Mitch immediately posted the notice and then went to inform Mrs. Johnson what had been decided (and to pick up the half pound of pecan divinity).

The store meeting was conducted on Saturday morning, and there were many full-time workers who volunteered to work for the students. When Mitch worked out the schedule, all the students except one could attend. The one who couldn't worked in the drapery department; her name was Ginger.

Ginger was a popular, pretty high school senior who really knew the drapery department merchandise, including the complicated hardware. Mitch went to see her when she came to work that evening.

"Ginger, I have some bad news for you," Mitch said.

"What is it?" she asked seriously.

"We tried to get a volunteer to work for you so you could get off to go to the homecoming, but no one could exchange with you. Mrs. Hanson wanted to, but she's going out of town and simply won't be here."

Ginger looked disappointed. "Thanks for trying," she said. "I understand, and I do appreciate the fact that you tried."

"You're quite welcome; however, that's not the bad news."

"It isn't? It must be really bad then." She looked at Mitch with such concern that it made him laugh.

"The bad news is that I'm going to work for you on Friday night. I'm studying my test for the drapery department, and with a little help from you on the hardware items, I'm confident I can help the ladies with their drapery needs."

Ginger was elated. She instantly jumped, put her arms around Mitch's neck and squeezed him in a tight, appreciative hug. "Thank you! Thank you!" she joyfully exclaimed.

"That will get us both fired," Mitch said while backing away. He looked around the store to see if customers were watching. "I don't mind working, and it will give me some time to work on my drapery department test."

The event night came, and the store was covered by full-time employees who wanted to give the students a chance to attend the homecoming. The volunteers felt good about being able to help, and the students were definitely grateful. It

53

was a win–win situation, and the following week, Mitch passed the test on the drapery department.

One Saturday morning several weeks after the homecoming, Mitch was passing the candy department, and he was stopped by Mrs. Johnson.

"I need to talk with you," she said seriously. "Something is bothering me, and I don't want to be a tattletale, but you need to be aware of it."

"Okay. I know you're not a tattletale; what is it?"

"It's Mrs. Davis, the cashier," Mrs. Johnson whispered. "She leaves her drawer open most of the time. Have you ever noticed?"

"No, I haven't," he admitted. "But I'll certainly keep my eyes open. Thanks."

Mrs. Davis was a tall, slender, very intelligent lady who was the most competent cashier in the store. She could ring almost twice as many customers through in a day as any other employee. She was good with the customers—fast and efficient—and her register always balanced to the penny. Her accuracy was almost unbelievable. That's why Mrs. Johnson's comment didn't bother Mitch. She was fast, she was accurate, and she always balanced.

A few days later, Mitch was in front of the check-outs making a list of bags that needed to be restocked when he noticed that Mrs. Davis had a line of customers at her register, and she was quickly ringing and completing transactions. But Mrs. Johnson was right. She was not closing the register drawer after each sale.

When there were no more customers at the register, Mitch approached her. "Why do you leave your register drawer open between transactions?" he asked. He heard a click as the drawer shut.

Mrs. Davis looked startled for an instant, then smiled confidently. "It's faster," she replied. "It saves time, and I can wait on more customers. That means better customer service and less payroll—that's good for the company. I like to see how many customers I can check out in a day."

"I appreciate your effort. You're very conscientious, and I'm delighted that you want to save the company money—that's very commendable. But company policy says that the drawer will be closed after each transaction, and I want you to follow company policy. Okay?"

"Okay, I was just trying to help."

"I know you were—please don't take offense. It is policy, and we must do it that way."

Mitch made it a point to check on her several times after that, and the drawer was always shut. "That problem was solved quickly and easily. I wish they were all that easy," he thought.

Several weeks later Mitch was passing the candy department when Mrs. Johnson called to him again.

"Mr. Andrews, I need to see you for a moment."

"Sure, what can I do for you?"

"Come around here. I want to show you something."

Mitch went behind the candy counter to where Mrs. Johnson was bending over the candy ordering book, and Mitch leaned over to look at some numbers she was pointing at.

"She's still doing it," Mrs. Johnson said in a very low voice, almost whispering. "When she sees you coming, she closes the drawer, but the rest of the time she leaves it open."

"Wow! Those are remarkable sales," Mitch said loud enough for Mrs. Davis to hear at the front. "But why?" Mitch whispered.

"I don't know, but I did hear you ask her to keep it closed, and she's not doing it."

"Thanks," Mitch said softly. "If you keep that up you're going to have the largest volume candy department in the company. Keep up the good work," he said loudly as he walked away.

Mitch went straight to see Mr. Courtney, and he informed him of everything that had happened.

"This is different than a lot of situations you have handled in the past," Courtney began. "Everyone will not always obey the rules; that's why you have to have a philosophy to deal with them. Whenever you have a large company, you must have rules—and when you have rules, you will always have someone who wants to break them. When that happens, it is up to responsible management to deal with the violation. That's why I adopted the philosophy 'firm but fair.' It means that I am firm in maintaining company policies and procedures, and fair in dealing with those who have defied those rules. I treat everyone the same, whether it's the receiving clerk or the manager of the restaurant—all are treated the same when it comes to company policy. Not only is it the right thing to do, but it will also keep you out of court on charges of discrimination."

"I agree with your philosophy," Mitch said, "but I'm not quite sure how I should handle this particular situation."

"The first thing we must do is to check her drawer. Get another cashier to open as soon as you shut Mrs. Davis' register down. If she is playing with the money, her drawer may be over. She would probably wait until near the end of her shift to take what she skimmed."

"Are you serious?" Mitch asked in disbelief.

"Absolutely! If her drawer is not over, I'll have her checked by professionals. There is a company called Will-Check that specializes in checking retail stores. They send unidentified shoppers to make purchases, and part of what they do is to check the cash register procedures. She couldn't prepare for them."

Mitch walked to the front of the store with Miss Tulip and pulled the cash drawer from Mrs. Davis' register.

"I need to borrow your drawer to verify something," Mitch said calmly. "We've opened another register, so why don't you take a break for a few minutes."

"What's going on?" Mrs. Davis asked. She was upset.

"I just need to verify something," Miss Tulip answered.

Mrs. Davis stormed to the break room in a huff.

Mitch watched as Miss Tulip counted the money, the checks, the charges, and finally balanced the cash register on the register report.

"It's twenty-seven dollars over," Miss Tulip commented to Mitch. "That's the first time in two years that she has been off a penny."

"Count it again, just to make sure," Mitch instructed, and he went to inform Mr. Courtney.

"She has to go!" Courtney said. "Have Miss Tulip sit in as your witness. Terminate her for 'improper cash-handling procedures.' She was obviously not following procedures, or her drawer would not be over. Be sure you get a written statement from Mrs. Johnson, and you write one which documents the time and date that you instructed her to keep her drawer closed."

"How could she be over and still balance every day?"

"She was not ringing some sales—ones that were easy to remember or tally—say, sales of even dollars that she could add quickly. Then, at the end of the shift, she would take the money that had not been rung on the register and turn in the rest. The register balanced; she had earned thirty to a hundred dollars extra, and no one knew the difference. She was very sharp."

"What if we made a mistake somewhere in our calculations?"

"The numbers should be carefully checked," Courtney stated.

"Miss Tulip is doing that now."

"Then there will be no mistake. She has been balancing registers for me for eight years. The only mistake made was by Mrs. Davis. She thought she would never get caught."

Mitch got everything prepared and called Mrs. Davis to his office. Miss Tulip was there as a witness.

"Mrs. Davis," Mitch began. "We have a problem."

Mrs. Davis was tense as she sat across from Mitch. Her posture was defiant. "You're right! We do have a problem when you just come up unannounced and pull my drawer in the middle of the day. I don't like being treated that way."

Mitch was nervous. He was inexperienced in this type of direct confrontation. "We have a serious problem," he repeated, not knowing exactly how to proceed.

"What is this big problem?" Mrs. Davis asked insolently. "First you pull my register and send me on break in the middle of the day, and then you call me to your office to tell me there is a problem. Well, I'll tell you—there *is* a problem." Her voice grew louder. "The problem is you treat people like you own them. It doesn't hurt to be courteous. But no—you have to walk all over your employees—treat them like dirt. That's the problem." Her eyes flashed as she talked.

"Why is your register twenty-seven dollars over?" Mitch asked. He tried to sound firm and in control—even though his heart was thumping so loudly he was certain everyone could hear it.

"It is not over! You can't count. You must have put that money in there on the way to the office." She sounded stressed, betraying her anxiety.

"Miss Tulip was with me the entire time. I could not have put the money in without her seeing it. Why would I want to do that, anyhow?"

"To get rid of me! You don't like me," she shouted.

"And the money was counted twice by Miss Tulip; she counts it every day. There is no mistake—your register is twenty-seven dollars over."

"There was a customer who gave me a fifty-dollar bill, and maybe I gave her change for a twenty. That would account for it."

"There was no fifty-dollar bill in your drawer," Miss Tulip interrupted.

"I'm going to have to let you go," Mitch said firmly, and he waited for her to explode.

"For what?!"

"For not following cash-handling procedures," Mitch said in a calm, firm voice. He was surprised at how calm he sounded. "Will you please sign this termination form which states that you were terminated for failure to follow proper cash-handling procedures?"

"Hell no!" she shouted. "You can stick that form where the sun doesn't shine. I quit! I wouldn't work for this stinking company one more minute." She stormed out of the office and went to clean out her locker.

"I'm going to write in the signature space that the employee refused to sign," Mitch said as he wrote on the form. "And now, Miss Tulip, if you will witness here," he said, placing an X where she was to sign. "And I'll sign and date it here. Thanks for your help."

"You handled that very professionally," she complimented.

"Thanks, that was the first time I ever terminated anyone, and I was a little nervous."

"It didn't show. I'm going to tell Mr. Courtney how well you handled it."

"Thanks. I guess that about does it," he said. Then he headed for Mr. Courtney's office.

"She quit!" Mitch announced as he walked into Mr. Courtney's office. "She blew up when I told her I was going to terminate her. She refused to sign the termination document, but Miss Tulip and I both signed it."

"You don't need her signature," Mr. Courtney assured. "You handled it perfectly. Your 'firm but fair' philosophy paid off today. It saved the company lots of money. If she already had twenty-seven dollars skimmed by midday, she must have been stealing fifty to a hundred dollars a day."

"Wow! She was making more than me."

"She was very clever. She had a good education, a good mind, and she was a very likeable person. She could have gone on for years and we would never have caught her. You handled that situation extremely well."

"Thank you! I really appreciate your comments."

"There's a valuable lesson in this," he said. "One you should focus on and remember. This 'wad' day is different! It's because you did something right for a change." He smiled to let Mitch know he was teasing. "Now write the following: I will deal with my employees using a FIRM BUT FAIR policy—being firm in maintaining compliance with company policy, procedure, and objectives, and fair in making decisions which impact those who report to me."

Mitch wrote as he was instructed, tore off the writing, and folded it into a tiny wad. He placed it in his pocket. "I hope I don't have to go through a situation like that again," he said.

"You will, I assure you, if you stay in the retail business. Situations like that will happen many times during your career. And you will handle them professionally."

Mitch returned to his office. He felt really good about the day and how he had handled the sensitive situation with Mrs. Davis. He was pleased with the positive strokes he received from Nat Courtney. Then he smiled. "I have an idea that will surprise him." He took a sheet of paper and a magic marker and wrote on the paper: I will deal with my employees using a 'firm but fair' policy—being firm in maintaining compliance with company policy, procedure, and objectives, and fair in making decisions which impact those who report to me."

"Just this once, I would like to be one step ahead of him." He placed the paper in the middle of his clean desk and went home.

8

For Mitch Andrews, the time seemed to fly. He was orchestrating a continuous transition from one season to the next. The store was being set up for Valentine's day; then Easter; next, it was summer, and then back-to-school. During that time, Mr. Courtney called Mitch to his office almost every morning to show him something useful—some little method or way to gain a little more profit to be a little more effective. They always seemed to be small and insignificant unto themselves; however, Mr. Courtney thought them important enough to take his time to show them to Mitch.

One day, Mitch learned how to pick up five points in margin by taking a regular purchase order for basic merchandise and combining it with a special purchase order for sale-event merchandise which had a cost of five percent less than the basic everyday price.

Then there was the time that Mr. Courtney showed him how to recover transportation charges on a split shipment of men's shirts. The store had ordered forty-eight dozen shirts, and the manufacturer had shipped them in two shipments of twenty-four dozen shirts each. Transportation charges were paid on both shipments. Mr. Courtney filed an "improper transportation claim" and charged the transportation costs on the second shipment back to the manufacturer.

Mitch had learned a lot from Mr. Courtney. Over the months, he had been watching and waiting to learn about the big things Mr. Courtney did to turn in an eleven percent pre-tax profit. One morning while he was in Mr. Courtney's office, it dawned on him that Nat Courtney was actually showing him how he did it. There wasn't any "big thing" after all—just a lot of little things performed on a daily basis which, over the course of a year, amounted to a monumental difference in the profitability of the store.

"Mr. Courtney," Mitch said one morning as Nat was showing him how to make extra profit on Easter baskets. "When I first came here, I watched you like a hawk to discover the 'big secret' you have that has enabled you to turn in such an astonishing profit. It's taken me all this time to realize what your big secret is. The secret is that there really is not a big secret! The hundreds of little things you do on a daily basis make a difference and, over the course of a year, cumulatively, they make a substantial difference."

"That's the secret all right!" Courtney grinned. He leaned back in his swivel chair and lit his pipe. He looked pleased that Mitch had made the comment. "Everyone looks for the obvious. It's all the little opportunities we have which can make a significant improvement in profit."

Mitch was not sure whether Nat Courtney was proud of himself for having finally taught him the secret of his success, or if he was proud of Mitch for having learned. In any event, it was a moment that Mitch would always savor.

Christmas came; then the white sale and inventory, and it was time for Valentine's Day again with Easter following close behind. Mitch had completed all the tests and projects required in the management training program. He was applying what he had learned, and the store was headed for another great year.

Mitch was busy overseeing the preparation of Easter displays when two distinguished-looking gentlemen, very expensively dressed, came up to him and introduced themselves as the Vice President of Finance, Mr. Counsel, and the Vice President of Personnel, Mr. Yates. They were from the M. G. Broad corporate office, and they wanted to see Mr. Courtney.

"I'm Mitch Andrews, Mr. Courtney's assistant. He's out for lunch right now. He'll be back in about an hour. Would you like to tour our store while you're waiting?"

"We'd love to," Mr. Counsel replied. "You lead the way."

Mitch was a knowledgeable host. Information flowed from him like a fountain. He showed them how the use of one color on all the mannequins throughout the store brought an ambiance of unity; how the placement of gum-label tickets on the inside of purses, in addition to the string tags on the outside, could foil a would-be ticket-switcher; how the shower curtains were displayed by color, and an extra shelf had been added to display the shower curtain rings which coordinated with them. He showed them a line of men's slacks which sold better—and at a higher margin—than the ones recommended by the buying office.

For every question the two vice presidents posed, Mitch had an appropriate answer, and the hour passed so quickly that Mitch was surprised when Mr. Courtney joined them.

"Did Mitch take care of you?" Nat asked.

"You bet he did," Mr. Yates replied. "We really enjoyed the tour."

The vice presidents and Mr. Courtney went to Nat's office where they spent a couple of hours. As soon as they departed, Mitch hurried back to Mr. Courtney's office to see how the visitors had liked the store.

"How did it go?" he asked Mr. Courtney.

"They both loved you!" he said with a smile. "You made a big hit."

"I just showed them around the store," Mitch replied, "but I'm glad they liked me."

"It was a very good visit. You don't get many like that in a career," he said while savoring the moment.

"I'd like to put a memo on the bulletin board to compliment all of our employees, and to let them know how much our distinguished visitors liked the store."

"Good idea! I'll write one from both of us."

Several weeks after the vice presidents visit, Mitch was paged to Mr. Courtney's office. As he entered, Nat motioned for him to sit down—it was going to be a long meeting.

"Mitch," he began, "you've learned a lot since you've been here. You're one of the best trainees I've ever had—and believe me, there have been a lot."

"Thanks," Mitch responded, "that means a lot to me, coming from you." He was flattered by the praise.

"There's one more important topic I'd like to cover with you," Courtney said solemnly. "It's probably the most difficult to cover because it is more abstract than the other topics we've discussed. It's about how to deal with your success as a manager if you achieve a noticeable degree of accomplishment in your career. You see, it's so easy to get caught up in a job, a position, a title—in the 'hunger of ambition,' that it's possible to be extremely successful in the eyes of other people, and yet be a complete failure. You can have position, power, money, and prestige, and still be miserable. I know people who earn incredible incomes—hold positions much higher than mine—and who are always comparing themselves to others who have risen higher, accomplished more, earned more. And the more they compare, the harder they strive, and the more frustrated they become. They are miserable; they're not satisfied with themselves, their families, or their accomplishments."

"I can see how that could happen," Mitch replied, still not certain about where the conversation was going.

"I've seen it many times over the years," Courtney continued. He was staring straight ahead, almost like he was in a trance, as he continued his monologue. "I've seen men ignore the needs of their families, betray their friends, and get caught up in a web of corporate power and politics that consumed them. They lose perspective and their lives become empty and meaningless. When I was a young store manager, I had a beautiful wife, and two wonderful children, a boy and a girl. I was eager for advancement. I pushed myself to learn, to perform, and to earn as much as I could to provide for those I loved so much. But I did take time—quality time—to spend with them; I can't begin to tell you how much I enjoyed my family. One night in January, I was working very late during inventory, and I received a telephone call from my neighbor. 'You'd better come home,' he said. 'Your house is on fire.' "

He looked at Mitch as if he was having second thoughts about continuing the story, and after a pause, he continued. "When I arrived, the fire trucks were already there. A crowd had gathered to watch the firemen battle the inferno that was raging in what was my home. I searched the crowd frantically for my family. I called their names, asked neighbors if they had seen them—all the while the terror was growing inside me. They were nowhere to be found. I stood watching the horror of the fire, and I realized that they were still inside."

Courtney took a deep breath; he looked as if he was going to cough—but he didn't, and he let the air slowly escape. He sat silent for a moment and began to speak again. "When the sun sets each day, for some people it sets for the last time. To me every sunrise is a wonder—another day that we have been given to enjoy, to savor—and I am thankful. I'm thankful that I've been given one more day in which I can live, be happy, love my family, and accomplish useful things for myself and others. I don't worry about what I don't have, who has more, or who has accomplished more. I appreciate the life I have been given. I eventually married again—a wonderful woman—and I have a daughter who is the apple of my eye. I enjoy my wife, my daughter, my job, my life—to the fullest."

"Thanks for sharing that with me," Mitch said. He felt privileged that Mr. Courtney had shared such personal details.

"I hope you will learn to put as much effort into—and derive as much satisfaction from—your family as you do your work."

Mr. Courtney completely changed his personality in the next second from solemn to jovial. "This is a 'wad' day," he said becoming more playful.

"Do you want me to write something?" Mitch asked. "It's been a long time since I've had to do that."

"Not this time," Courtney replied. "I wrote this one for you."

He reached in his desk drawer and pulled out what appeared to be a framed picture. He stared at it through the spectacles perched on his nose and began to read. "Number seven. I will be thankful that I have been given this day in which I can accomplish so much." He handed it to Mitch.

It was not a picture, but a series of affirmations which had been typeset on elegant paper. They were entitled the "I wills." They were the very principles he had forced Mitch to write on pieces of paper and carry in his pocket until he remembered them. It was beautifully framed, and Mitch was deeply touched by the gift.

"Mr. Courtney, I don't know how to thank you," Mitch said as he admired the piece. "I can't tell you how much this means to me."

"I have one more gift for you," he said smiling. "You're the new store manager at the Highlands store."

Mitch was shocked.

"When do I start?" he asked. The full impact had not yet hit him.

"Monday."

"Do you know anything about that store?"

"I know quite a bit about it," Courtney began, and he spent the next hour briefing Mitch on the previous manager, the area, and how he should go about establishing himself as the new manager.

That evening, Mitch was standing near the front of the store, and he noticed that there was a magnificent sunset. He thought of the wonderful day he had experienced, about his beautiful wife at home waiting for him, the experience he had gained at this store, and all that Mr. Courtney had taught him—and he was thankful.

9

The new trainee entered Mitch's office and extended his hand. "I'm Jack Duvall," he said. "I'm your new management trainee."

"I'm Mitch Andrews," Mitch said politely as he looked the new trainee over from head to toe. "Have a seat."

"You look awfully young to be a training store manager," Jack commented as he seated himself.

"Perhaps," Mitch replied. "I had an excellent teacher."

"Who was that?"

"Nat Courtney, in Arlington."

"I hear he's tough," Jack said. "I'm glad I didn't get assigned to his store."

Mitch grinned. "He's tough all right—but he produces more profit than any other store in the company. Come on. I'll show you to your office. You get settled, and I'll be by at nine-thirty to take you around the store and introduce you to everyone. If you need anything, let me know."

"Thanks, Mr. Andrews. I look forward to working with you."

At nine-thirty, Mitch went by Jack's office and took him around the store, and introduced him to the staff. He then gave Jack a complete orientation which covered everything from the personnel paperwork to the establishment of a training calendar.

About a week later, Mitch paged Jack to come to his office. "Where is the report that was due today on hardware?"

"I'll have it for you in a minute," Jack said, and he dashed off to his office to find it.

After about thirty minutes, Mitch walked to Jack's office to see what was keeping him. As he walked into the office, Jack was frantically digging through a pile of messy papers on his desk.

"I'm having a little trouble locating it," he said. "I'll have it in just a minute."

"This will not do!" Mitch said sternly. "This simply will not do. What is that all over your desk?"

"My paperwork," Jack replied. Little beads of perspiration started popping out on his forehead as he frantically dug through the overabundance of unorganized documents on his desk.

"We need to talk," Mitch said. "Come to my office."

Mitch sat behind his desk and Jack sat across from him.

"You're going to have to come over here if you want to learn," Mitch said as he pulled the drawer open which contained his one to thirty-one file.

"This is what I call my memory."